At the Park

This Green Light Reader belongs to:

_____

I read it by myself on:

_____

At the Park

A Mr. and Mrs. Green
Adventure

KEITH BAKER

Green Light Readers
HOUGHTON MIFFLIN HARCOURT
Boston   New York

The text of this book is set in Giovanni Book.
The illustrations were done in acrylic paint on illustration board.

The Library of Congress has cataloged *More Mr. and Mrs. Green* as follows:
Baker, Keith.
More Mr. and Mrs. Green/Keith Baker.
p. cm.
ISBN: 978-0-15-216494-2 hardcover
ISBN: 978-0-15-205246-1 paperback
Summary. Mr. and Mrs. Green, two alligators, spend time together fishing, painting,
and going to the park.
[1. Fishing—Fiction. 2. Jellybeans—Fiction. 3. Painting—Fiction. 4. Parks—Fiction.
5. Alligators—Fiction.] I. Title.
PZ7.B17427Mo 2004
[Fic]—dc21 2002011385

ISBN: 978-0-544-55556-3 GLR paperback
ISBN: 978-0-544-55557-0 GLR paper over board

Manufactured in China
SCP 10 9 8 7 6 5 4 3 2 1

4500569291

For Laurie,

with great,

green gratitude

"I won, I won, I won!" said Mr. Green.

"First to the fountain."

He did a little victory dance.

Mrs. Green was not racing.

She was standing in the middle

of Emerald Garden.

"Look, look, look!" she said.

"So many butterflies—

graceful swallowtails . . .

 magnificent monarchs . . .

glorious painted ladies . . .

They're dazzling!"

Mr. Green was not looking.

He was walking across
the monkey bars—
on his hands.
"Watch this!"

Mr. Green did a double
back flip onto the grass.
"A perfect 10!" he said.

Mrs. Green was not watching.

She was listening to the birds.

"So many songs!" said Mrs. Green.

"Robins warbling . . .

sparrows chirping . . .

chickadees peeping . . .

It's like a symphony!"

Mr. Green was not listening.

He was swimming
back and forth
across the wading pool—
77 times.

"A new world record!"
said Mr. Green.
He raised his arms
in triumph.

Mrs. Green did not see him.

Her nose was in the flowers.

"Ahhh . . ." she said.

"The sweet lilies . . .

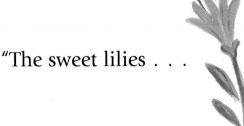

the spicy daisies . . .

the perfumey roses . . .

They smell good enough to—"

Mrs. Green stopped.
She heard a sound.
She listened closely.

Mr. Green stopped.
He heard the
same sound.

It was one of their favorite sounds—

better than a cuckoo clock,

better than a train whistle,

even better than a marching band.

It was . . .

ding-a-ling ding ding ding

the bell on the ice cream truck!

Mrs. Green looked at Mr. Green.

"First one there is the winner!" she said.

"Ready . . . set . . . go!"

They took off in a flash.

Mr. Green's stride was long—

for an alligator.

He pulled ahead.

Mrs. Green veered to the left.

She had a plan.

Mr. Green ran

under the rings,

around the merry-go-round,

22

through the frog pond,

over the footbridge,

and down the final stretch.

But Mrs. Green was already there.
(She had taken the secret shortcut.)

"I got chocolate Bucko Bammo Bars,"
she said, "with nuts!"
"Yummm . . ." said Mr. Green,
"my favorite."

Mrs. Green ate her bar slowly,
in 97 licks and 33 nibbles.

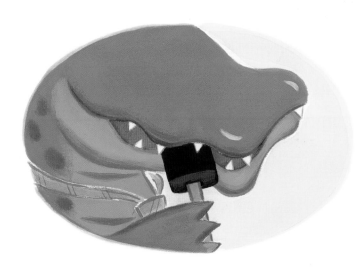

Mr. Green ate his bar quickly,
in 6 big sloppy bites.
(He finished first,
but it was not a race.)

Mr. Green was still hungry—
so was Mrs. Green.
"Let's go home and
make spaghetti," he said.
"With mashed potatoes!" she said.

Mrs. Green took Mr. Green's hand.
"And on the way home," she said,
"we might see a purple-spotted dragonfly."
"Or perhaps . . ." said Mr. Green,

". . . another ice cream truck!"

About the Author

Keith Baker has written and illustrated many well-loved picture books and beginning readers, including several about the charming and lovable Mr. and Mrs. Green. He lives in Seattle, Washington. Visit his website at www.KeithBakerBooks.com.

More Green Light Readers starring
Mr. and Mrs. Green!

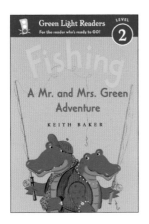

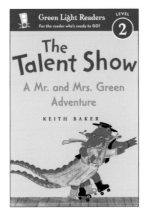

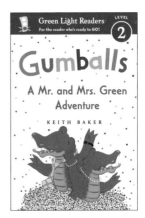

More reading fun with great characters in favorite Green Light Readers series!

LEVEL 2

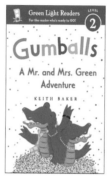

LEVEL 3

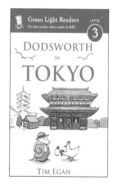